THE ADVENTURES OF

Daisy & Tom

THE TEDDY BEARS' PICNIC

Story by Rosie Alison

Pictures by Atholl McDonald

BLOOMSBURY
CHILDREN'S
BOOKS

For Lucy & Daisy: R.A.
For Cairn & Brodie: A.M.

First published in Great Britain in 1999 by
Bloomsbury Publishing Plc, 38 Soho Square, London, W1V 5DF

Copyright © Text Rosie Alison

Illustrations by Atholl McDonald

The moral right of the author has been asserted.
A CIP catalogue record of this book is available from
the British Library.

ISBN: 0 7475 3856 5

Printed and bound in Hong Kong

10 9 8 7 6 5 4 3 2 1

Daisy and Tom are twins with a
wonderful secret: they have a magic kite
called Oscar, who carries them off on
adventures to mysterious new lands.

Time and again they set off
knowing that Oscar will always bring them
safely back home in the end.

This particular adventure began
on a bright winter's day, when the fields were
white with snow...

It was a frosty morning, and the twins were busy
polishing their sledge. Daisy looked up and noticed
that Bing, their teddy bear, was sitting by the door.

"How did Bing get there?" she asked.

"*I* didn't move him," said Tom.

"I sometimes think Bing goes off somewhere
when nobody is looking," muttered Daisy.

Later that morning, their mother's freshly baked flapjacks went missing.

"Where can they have got to?" she sighed. Daisy and Tom *promised* that they hadn't eaten them.

Something strange was going on - and Daisy began to suspect that Bing was somehow involved.

After lunch, the twins settled down to play with their Christmas train set. All was peaceful until Daisy spotted something moving outside the window ...

"Quick, Tom," she cried, "it's Bing out there - we must follow him!"

The twins pulled on their coats and ran outside, clutching their magic kite. They could just see Bing Bear hurrying through the fields. He seemed to be carrying something tied in one of Daisy's red handkerchieves.

Once through their garden gate, the twins lost sight of Bing altogether. Where could he have gone? Oscar carried them high over the fields, so they could search the ground below.

"Over there!" called Tom. Far away, they spotted Bing hurrying into Conker Wood.

But by the time they reached Conker Wood, Bing had vanished again. The twins wandered through a maze of trees, until Oscar tugged them to look round.

"There he is!" cried Daisy. Sure enough, they just glimpsed Bing scurrying through the darkness.

Bing hurried over to a huge oak tree, and clambered up the lower branches. The twins crept along behind him, and were just in time to see him knock three times on a little door in the tree trunk. The door opened and Bing disappeared inside.

Daisy and Tom climbed up the tree until they came to the hidden door. They knocked three times, and were astonished when the door opened on to a strange dark passage ...

The twins stepped through the door and whooosh! - they found themselves slipping down a long dark slide until they landed with a bump at a little red door ...

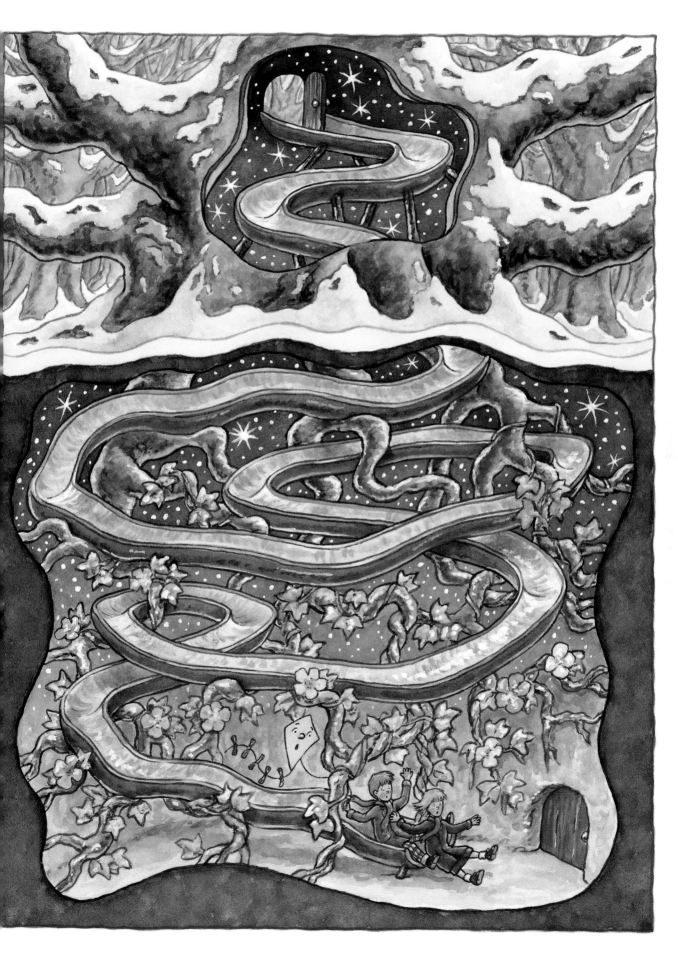

The door opened on to the most astonishing springtime world. It was a sunny land of beehives and giant flowers and streams of running honey ...

Almost at once, they bumped into their teddy bear. Poor Bing was so surprised to see the twins that he dropped his red handkerchief and out tumbled their mother's flapjacks.

"We won't tell," laughed Daisy, making it clear that they weren't angry.

"I just had to bring *something* to the Teddy Bears' Picnic," said Bing. He soon explained that they had come to a secret land where the bees and the bears worked together - the teddy bears had made a wonderful garden for the bees, and the bees gave them honey in return.

"Once a year, we all gather together for a great picnic party - why don't you join us?" asked Bing. He pointed towards a pleasant wood in the distance where the picnic would be held. The twins took off their winter coats, and were all set to follow Bing, when a pretty bee came buzzing over with a message.

"Please come and help us!" she hummed. "Poor Rufus Bear is trying to carry our special honey cake, and it's much too big for him!" At once, Bing and the twins followed the bee, whose name was Dizzy.

Sure enough, they found poor Rufus tottering under an enormous beehive of a cake. Oscar flew to the rescue, pulling the cake upright, whilst the twins helped to lift it on to Rufus's wheelbarrow.

"That's going to be some cake!" said Bing, admiring the great tower of honeycombs.

Rufus mixed the icing, and they all helped to decorate the cake ...

… they made sugar flowers ...

… and marzipan bears ...

… then they wrapped it all up in a large box with ribbons, ready for the Teddy Bears' Picnic.

They were running a little late for the picnic, so Bing suggested that they catch a lift by boat. He led them down to a jetty, and it wasn't long before a cheery Sailor Bear appeared with a colourful tug boat.

Sailor Bear carried them all off down the honey river. They chugged their way through magical gardens, dotted with beehive houses and towering flowers. All along the river bank, they watched the honey bees at work, flying from blossom to blossom.

But their chatterbox captain was so busy pointing out all the sights that he stopped watching the river ahead and took a wrong turning.

"Look out!" called Tom, and they all turned round to see that they were heading straight for an enormous waterfall ...

At once, Oscar flew into action: he wrapped his string tight around the deck rail, and pulled the boat right back from the very brink of the waterfall. He was *just* in time.

S ailor Bear steered them safely back on course, and soon they were gliding gently towards the woods. Along the river bank, teddy bears of every kind were strolling towards the picnic, each carrying some food or drink. Sailor Bear moored the boat and the twins joined the throng of bears …

At last, hidden amongst the trees,
they found a glorious Teddy Bears' Picnic in full swing.
Bing passed around his flapjacks, and all the bears shared their
food - even the bees joined in. But when Rufus uncovered
the honey cake, everyone agreed that it was
the very prize of
the party ...

W hen the picnic was finally over, Bing Bear was
so tired that Daisy had to carry him home. Oscar
pulled them all the way up the tree slide
until they stepped once more into
the wintry coldness of Conker
Wood. Snow was falling as
they all flew back home ...

At last they reached their warm house. Their parents were peacefully reading the papers in the kitchen.

"I still can't help wondering where those flapjacks could have got to," sighed their mother. The children winked at Bing, and said no more.

They would never tell Bing's secret ...